Monarch!
Come PLAY
with Me

by Ba Rea

Bas Relief Publishing Group

*Dedicated to my dad, Norman H. Rea II,
who looked out for me when I was changing.*

*And thanks to my daughter Mindy King, my good friend
Camry Sidick, my friend Carol Cullar's grandson Sage
Cullar-Ledford and hundreds of monarchs, for being the
models for this book.*

Text and illustrations
© Ba Rea 2006
All Rights Reserved
Published by
Bas Relief Publishing Group, P.O. Box 426,
Glenshaw, PA 15116
http://www.basrelief.org

ISBN-13: 978-0-9657472-5-7
ISBN-10: 0-9657472-5-5
Library of Congress Control Number: 2005908540

Monarch!
Come play with me.

4

What is play?

5

I'll show you.
We'll have fun.

Hey!
What are
you doing?

8

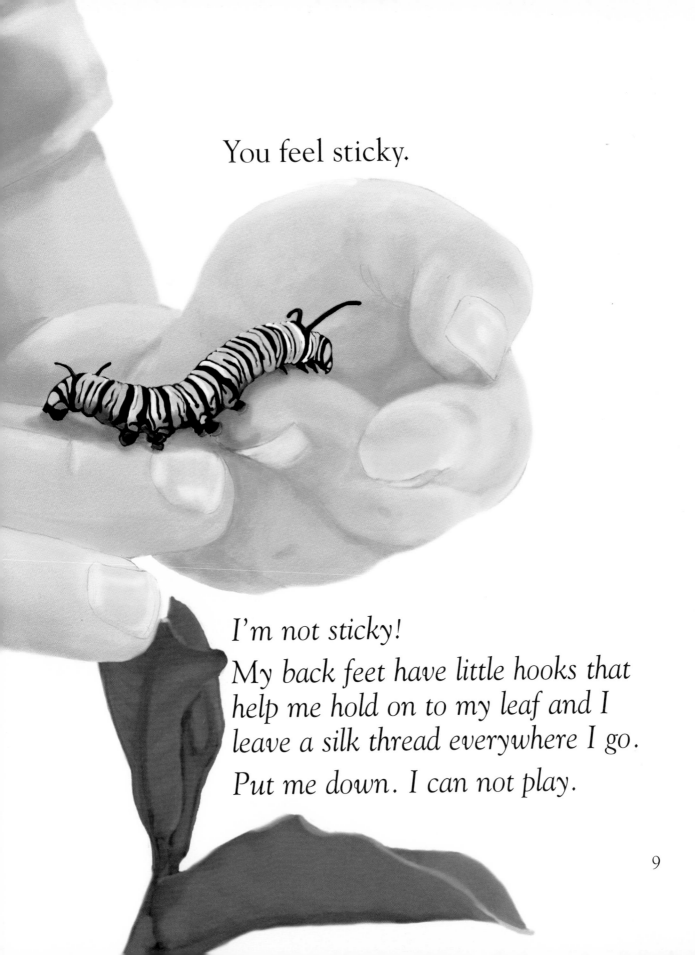

You feel sticky.

I'm not sticky!
My back feet have little hooks that help me hold on to my leaf and I leave a silk thread everywhere I go.
Put me down. I can not play.

9

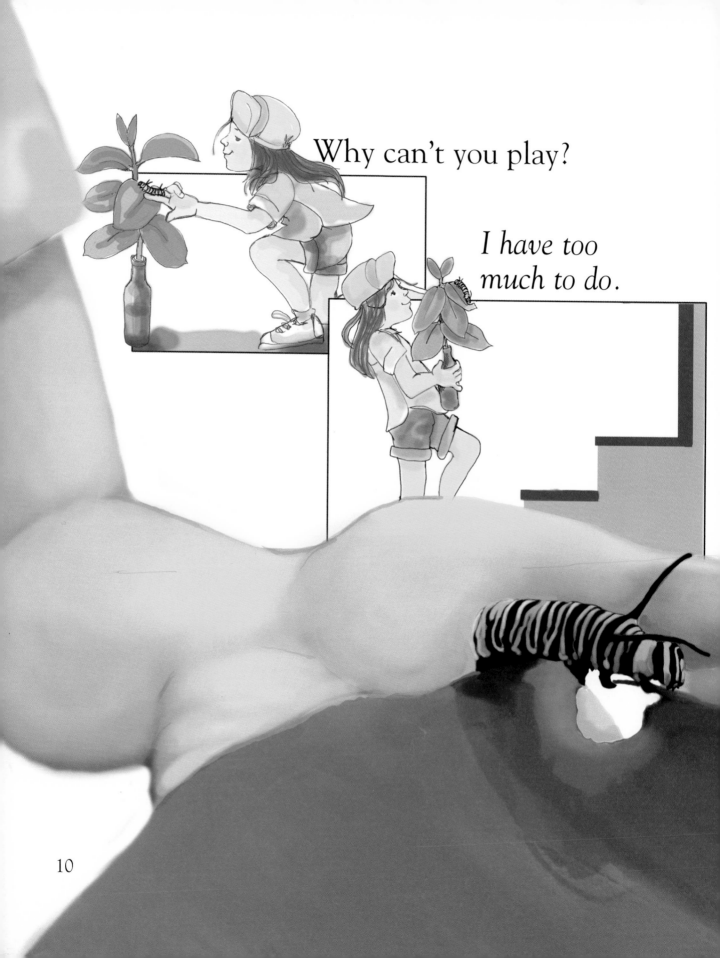

Why can't you play?

I have too much to do.

10

What do you have to do?

I must eat
and eat.

I eat too.

13

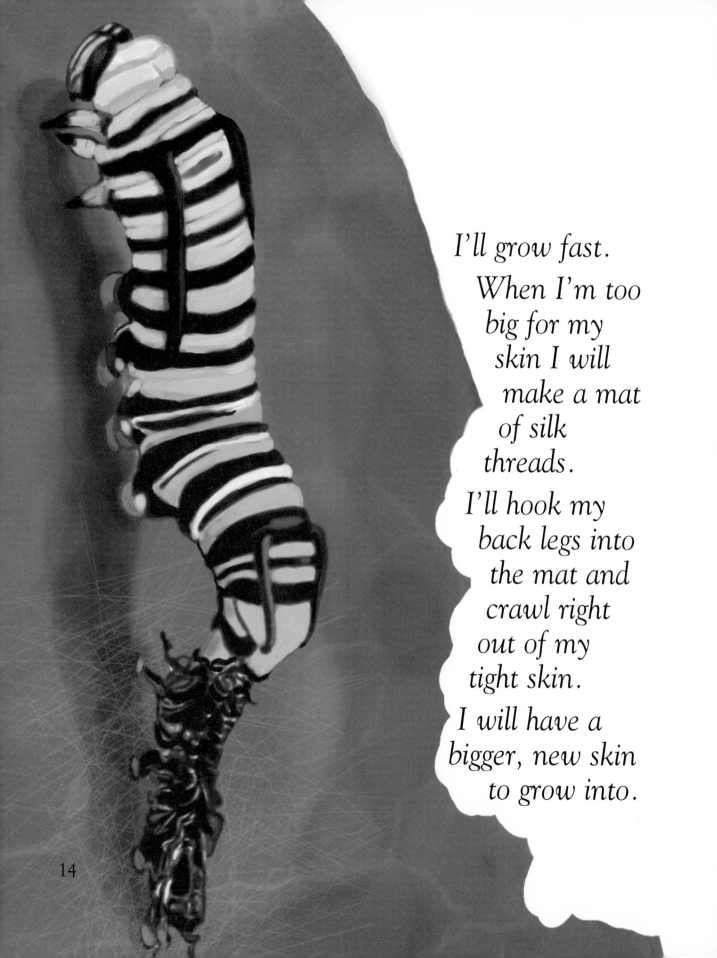

I'll grow fast. When I'm too big for my skin I will make a mat of silk threads.

I'll hook my back legs into the mat and crawl right out of my tight skin.

I will have a bigger, new skin to grow into.

14

I'm growing too.
Some of my clothes
are too small, but
my skin still fits.

15

I will eat only milkweed and I'll make lots of frass.

16

I eat peanut butter and jelly sandwiches, pickles and peaches.

Frass is a funny word, but I know what it means. Ha ha! Everybody poops.

When I'm big enough
I will look for
a special
place
to make
a sturdy
button with
my silk thread.

I'll hang by
my feet from the button
for a long time.

18

I can hang
by my feet
for a little
while.

19

When the time is right
I'll squeeze out of my skin.
I will wiggle and push to become
a chrysalis.

20

I don't know how to do that.
I will watch you.

21

I'll be very still,
but inside I will be changing.

When I come out
I will be very different.

I'll be very busy at school,
but I will look out for you.

24

You sure do look different.
Are you O.K.?

I must pump up my wings
before I can spread them wide.

I'll take you back
outside so you can fly.

I must fly high
and far away.

29

Goodbye.

I will remember you.

Where do monarch butterflies go in the fall?

In the northern United States and Canada we see many kinds of moths and butterflies in the summer. In winter there is no food for them and it is very cold. They must all find a way to survive.

Have you ever seen a woolly bear caterpillar? They hibernate under fallen leaves in the winter. In the spring, they make cocoons and then turn into Isabella moths. Swallowtail caterpillars pupate and hibernate as chrysalides all winter long. The butterflies emerge in the spring. Mourning cloak butterflies get out of the ice and snow by squeezing under the bark of trees. Monarchs migrate. They fly to a place that is not too cold and not too hot. They cluster together on trees for the winter. In the western United States, monarch butterflies cluster on trees in California near the Pacific Ocean. In the east they head south.

For a long time no one knew where the eastern monarchs went. In 1937, a scientist from Canada named Dr. Fred Urquhart and his wife Norah decided to find out. They put little tags on the wings of monarch butterflies heading south for the winter. Each tag had the Urquharts' address and a number to identify the butterfly. The Urquharts needed people to help them tag butterflies and look for butterflies that had been tagged. They put ads in newspapers all over North America. Thousands of people helped. They tagged butterflies and found many tagged butterflies to send back to Fred and Norah Urquhart. The Urquharts kept notes about where each butterfly was tagged and where it was found. They looked for clues to tell them where the monarchs were going.

It took a long time, but in 1976, the Urquharts and their helpers found out where the eastern monarchs go. They found millions of monarchs clustering on a mountainside in Mexico. The people living there knew that the butterflies came every year, but they did not know where they came from. Now we know that millions of monarchs from Canada and the United States go to Mexico for the winter. We all share the monarchs.

Today, school children from Mexico, the United States and Canada help scientists learn more about the monarch migration. They report their monarch migration observations to a program called **Journey North**. Some work with **Monarch Watch** to tag monarchs during the fall migration. Families monitor milkweed patches in their neighborhoods with the **Monarch Larva Monitoring Project**. Children also learn about monarchs and help scientists understand them better through organizations like **Monarchs in the Classroom** and **Lifestrands**.

****

Internet sites dedicated to supporting professional and student investigation of the monarch butterfly:

Journey North	http://www.learner.org/jnorth/
Lifestrands, Inc.	http://www.lifestrands.org
Monarchs in the Classroom	http://www.monarchlab.org
Monarch Larva Monitoring Project	http://www.mlmp.org
Monarch Watch	http://www.monarchwatch.org